MAGIC KEEPERS
CRYSTAL CHAOS

To my brilliant editors Mattie Whitehead and Karelle
Tobias who have both added so much to Magic Keepers
and who have made writing it so much fun! – L. C.

To the child who believes in magic – H. G.

STRIPES PUBLISHING LIMITED
An imprint of the Little Tiger Group
1 Coda Studios, 189 Munster Road, London SW6 6AW

Imported into the EEA by Penguin Random House Ireland,
Morrison Chambers, 32 Nassau Street, Dublin D02 YH68

A paperback original
First published in Great Britain in 2022

Text copyright © Linda Chapman, 2022
Illustration copyright © Hoang Giang, 2022

ISBN: 978-1-78895-440-2

The right of Linda Chapman and Hoang Giang to be identified as the author and
illustrator of this work respectively has been asserted by them in accordance with the
Copyright, Designs and Patents Act, 1988.

The Forest Stewardship Council® (FSC®) is a global, not-for-profit organization
dedicated to the promotion of responsible forest management worldwide. FSC defines
standards based on agreed principles for responsible forest stewardship that are supported
by environmental, social, and economic stakeholders. To learn more, visit www.fsc.org

10 9 8 7 6 5 4 3 2 1

MAGIC KEEPERS

CRYSTAL CHAOS

LINDA CHAPMAN
Illustrated by Hoang Giang

LITTLE TIGER
LONDON

CONTENTS

CHAPTER ONE

Ava pushed open the heavy door and peered into the enormous room. It had a high, domed ceiling with huge, old-fashioned windows that were framed by dusty velvet curtains. The October sun shone in through the dirty glass, casting patterns on the wooden floor and on the faded blue sofa at the far end of the room. There were bookcases crammed with leather-bound books, a large oak desk and a set of shelves filled with strange objects.

Pepper, Ava's Tibetan terrier, trotted inside,

her ears pricked.

"Stay close, Pepper," Ava said. Pepper ignored her and bounded straight to one of the windows, where she put her front paws on the windowsill and looked out. Ava grinned. She had taken Pepper to training classes when she'd been a puppy, but they'd been asked to leave because she wouldn't do as she was told. Ava didn't care though, she loved Pepper to bits and didn't mind that she was naughty – Ava wasn't always very good at doing what she was told either!

The door creaked shut behind her.

"It's seriously creepy in here, isn't it, Pepper?" Ava said, looking round at the vast room.

Ava's mum's great-aunt Enid had been a famous archaeologist who had worked all over the world and this room held her private collection of curios – unusual objects that she'd been given or had found over the years. When Great-Aunt Enid died, she had left the house to Ava's mum on the condition that the collection was to remain in the house and not be sold. In her will, she had said that although the curios were not particularly valuable she hoped one day one of her relatives would realize how special they were.

When Ava had asked her mum what they were going to do with the curios, her mum had just shrugged. "Heaven knows! I think I'll just leave them for now. There's so much else that needs sorting. The whole house needs redecorating and re-wiring."

Ava agreed that the house definitely needed a makeover. It was huge, with eight bedrooms spread over two upstairs floors, but the wallpaper was peeling off, the paintwork was chipped, and the rugs covering the wooden floors were threadbare. The kitchen hadn't been updated in a long time and outside was just as neglected. The garden was overgrown with rusty metal gates and a crumbling brick wall separating it from the street.

Ava, her mum and Pepper had moved into Curio House just a few days ago during Ava's half-term break. It was two hours away from their cosy, terraced house in Nottingham and Ava still felt like they were on holiday and would be going home soon.

It might start to feel more real when I go to school tomorrow, she thought. Ava was a little nervous about starting at a new school in Year Six when everyone already had their friends but she liked meeting new people so she hoped it would be OK.

Her footsteps echoed in the silent room as she approached the shelves that held the curios. The air was very still and she suddenly had the feeling she was being watched. Ava glanced over her shoulder but of course there was no one there. She smiled to herself. The room was really creeping her out!

The curios were all different shapes and sizes and each had a handwritten label. There was a chipped stone plaque carved with an ugly face, and an ornate metal goblet with strange markings; a fan with greying ostrich feathers; dusty figurines; pieces of old jewellery and a large, crouching stone gargoyle, among other things. Ava couldn't help feeling puzzled. Why had Great-Aunt Enid said the curios were special? They just looked old and broken to her.

Curiously, she picked up an object that was wrapped in old brown bandages. It was about fifty centimetres long with a flat dark snout poking out of one end. What was it? She was about to read the label when she heard a muffled noise behind her and swung round.

A-CHOO! Pepper backed out from behind one of the dusty curtains, sneezing.

Ava's shoulders relaxed. "Pepper! You made me jump!"

Pepper sneezed again, shook her head and trotted over to the desk. With her heart gradually slowing to normal speed, Ava read the label of the bandaged object she was holding: *Baby crocodile mummy. Ancient Egypt.*

A mummified crocodile – ick!

Hastily putting it down, she picked up a figurine with a human body and a cat head wearing a very stern expression. Ava grinned and waggled it from side to side. "What's the matter with you then?" she said. "Cat got your tongue?"

A pulse like a heartbeat throbbed through her fingers and she almost dropped the figurine in surprise. What had just happened? She stared at the figurine, waiting to see if the strange pulsing would happen again.

Nothing.

A shiver crossed her skin and she glanced uneasily at the rest of the curios. She had the sensation that they were watching her, waiting for something to happen.

Don't be a doughnut, she told herself firmly. *It's just one of your odd feelings. Ignore it.*

Ever since she'd been little she'd had strange

feelings about things. If she was in a forest she would feel as if the trees were trying to talk to her, or if she touched an animal she would instinctively know whether it was hurt or not. Her mum said it was because she was imaginative and intuitive but other people seemed to think it was weird so she'd learned not to talk about it.

CRASH!

Ava swung round but saw it was just Pepper again. The dog had jumped on to the desk, knocking a leather-covered box on to the floor. Putting the figurine down, Ava went over. "Oh, Pepper, you're such trouble!"

Pepper gave her a doggy smile, her fringe flopping over her face and her tongue hanging out.

Ava lifted her off the desk. "Come on, down you get."

Pepper licked Ava's chin and then wriggled out of her arms and trotted over to the curios.

Ava picked the box off the floor. There were some words in gold writing stamped into the leather lid.

"Mag…" she said, attempting to sound out the first word. "Mag-yck." Did it say *magic*? Ava was sure the word *magic* was spelled differently but she wasn't great at reading. She continued on. "Magyck Crystals for…" It looked like there had been some more words after 'for' but they had rubbed away.

A flicker of curiosity ran through Ava. Magyck crystals sounded interesting. *Though of course they won't really be magic*, she told herself quickly. *Magic isn't real. It must be some kind of game.*

Wondering why the box had been on the desk and not with the other curios, Ava opened the lid. Inside there was a grid of square compartments, each with a round, shiny crystal inside, nestling on a bed of purple silk. On the right-hand side of the grid there was a single, larger compartment of red silk with a big, oval stone – one side black and one side white – on the left-hand side there was a compartment of white silk that contained a gold necklace with a pendant, and below the grid was a compartment with a long, slim, clear crystal shaped like a pencil in it.

Someone had written notes on the inside of the box lid but the writing was tiny and Ava quickly gave up trying to read it. Instead, she picked up one of the crystals, a dark one with red patches. As her fingers closed on it, a powerful surge of energy rushed through her and when Pepper made a snuffling noise behind her, she found herself leaping high into the air. "Whoa!" she exclaimed, blinking in surprise. She was being seriously jumpy today!

Putting the crystal down, Ava felt the energy fade. Picking up another crystal, a glossy green one with a dark purple stripe, a wave of calm instantly fell over her. Her muscles relaxed, her breathing steadied and she found her chin lifting and her shoulders dropping.

It's the crystal. Ava's thoughts suddenly became clearer and more certain than they'd ever been before. *It's making me feel like this.*

She put it down, wondering what was going on. How could crystals change the way she was feeling? Her gaze fell on the black-and-white stone in the single red compartment. What would happen if she picked that one up?

The second Ava touched it, a chill prickled down her spine and she felt as though an army of spiders was running over her skin.

The sensation was so horrible that she dropped the stone and it thudded to the floor.

Ava was just steeling herself to pick it up so she could put it back in the box when she noticed Pepper going round in circles nearby with something in her mouth. Her shaggy tail was curled over her back and she was wagging it slowly from side to side, looking very pleased with herself.

"What have you got—?" Ava broke off as she saw a bandaged shape sticking out of Pepper's mouth. Oh no! It was the crocodile mummy!

"Pepper, you can't have that! Drop it!" she said in alarm, forgetting about the crystals for the moment.

Pepper gave her a look as if to say, *No, it's mine!*

"Pepper, I'm being serious. Come here," warned Ava, stepping towards her.

Brown eyes sparkling with mischief, the little terrier darted away!

CHAPTER TWO

"Pepper!" Ava called, chasing after the dog. "That's not a toy. Give it back!"

Pepper stopped in a play bow at the far end of the room, bottom in the air, her tail wagging.

Ava skidded to a halt too. She knew that if she charged, Pepper would race off again, thinking it was a game.

"Stay!" Ava said firmly, edging closer and wishing she'd worked harder on practising the obedience commands they'd learned in puppy training.

19

Still watching her, Pepper started to pull at the loose bandages. Ava gulped. Pepper loved to rip dog toys apart and she had a sudden, horrible image of the ancient crocodile mummy scattered around the room in tiny bits.

"Ava? Where are you?" Hearing her mum calling from the depths of the house, Ava froze. Although Mum didn't seem too bothered by the curios, Ava was sure she wouldn't be happy if she found Pepper chewing one!

"Pepper, give me that crocodile now," she hissed.

"Ava?"

"Just a minute, Mum!" Ava called desperately.

Giving up her 'approach cautiously' plan, she darted towards Pepper. Pepper jumped up but

20

Ava threw herself at the terrier and grabbed her collar. "Got you!" she said triumphantly. Pepper rolled on her back. Ava tried to pull the crocodile from her mouth but Pepper hung on tight.

"GRRR!" the dog play-growled, thinking it was a game.

Finally, Ava managed to prise the crocodile away and she scrambled to her feet just as the door opened.

"There you are, sweetie," her mum said. "It's easy to lose you in this house!"

"Hi, Mum," Ava said brightly, holding the now rather soggy crocodile mummy behind her back with one hand. Pepper danced around, trying to jump up to get at it.

"What have you been doing?" Mum asked, pushing back her hair. She and Ava looked very alike – they were both tall with eyes the colour of conkers and thick, dark hair. They shared the same hair and eye colouring as Ava's grandparents who were originally from

Italy. Ava's dad looked very different – he had sandy-blonde hair and green eyes. He and her mum had split up when Ava was just a baby and he now lived in the north of Scotland with his new wife and their baby son, Fergus. Ava saw him a few times a year when she went to stay with them in the school holidays, but most of the time she lived with her mum.

"Just looking round," said Ava innocently. She noticed the black-and-white stone lying on the floor near her feet. Pants! She hoped Mum wouldn't start asking questions about why it was out of its box. She quickly stepped in front of the stone to block it from her mum's sight. Ava was very curious about the strange crystals and the last thing she wanted was Mum saying they were not to be played with and deciding to take them away.

"Whatever's the matter with Pepper?" her mum said, looking at the terrier, who was still jumping up and down behind Ava.

"I don't know," said Ava, her voice coming out
as a squeak. "I think she needs a walk. I'll take
her out now."

"Great, could you call in at the corner
shop for me at the same time?" her mum said.
"We need onions and a tin of tomatoes for the
pasta sauce tonight."

"OK," gasped Ava as Pepper's teeth snapped
just below the mummy.

Her mum smiled. "Thanks, sweetie. I'll get
you some money." She turned away.

Sighing in relief, Ava quickly shoved the

crocodile on a shelf and scooped up the stone. As she touched it, an icy feeling swept over her. She hastily put it on the shelf beside the mummy and the strange feeling faded. "Come on, Pepper, walkies!" she said.

Pepper woofed happily and ran to the door.

With one last look at the box of mysterious crystals, Ava followed her out.

✦

Ava stopped at the shop at the end of their street and then crossed the main road and took Pepper for a run beside the river. The river wound its way through open parkland, heading into town in one direction and out into countryside in the other. Ava headed along the path towards town, throwing a ball for Pepper. Every time she threw it and told Pepper to fetch, Pepper looked at her as if to say, *You threw it, you get it!*

"Pepper, this is supposed to be fun for you," Ava said. "Dogs like to fetch." She threw the ball again. "Go on, go get it!" she encouraged.

Pepper turned and trotted off in the opposite direction.

Ava gave up and stuffed the ball in her coat pocket. Ahead of her there was a bridge where she could see two adults playing a game with a young boy and girl. They were throwing sticks in the water and then hurrying to the other side of the bridge to see whose stick came out first.

"Pepper, come here!" Ava called, not wanting Pepper to see them in case she decided to grab one of the sticks and run away with it. She might not like playing fetch but she did like being involved in anything fun that was going on! Ava took a packet of Pepper's favourite meaty dog treats out of her pocket – she always carried some, just in case she needed them. Hearing the packet rustle, Pepper came bounding over. Ava fed her a couple of treats and guided her away from the bridge. On a nearby bench, a girl was reading a thick book. She was wearing a padded pink coat and had a woolly hat over her long dark hair. She was turning the pages quickly, her eyes skimming easily over the words. *How can she read that fast?* Ava thought as she got closer.

Pepper trotted over to say hello. The girl exclaimed in surprise as Pepper jumped up and put her muddy paws on the girl's knees.

"I'm sorry!" Ava called, breaking into a run. "Pepper! Down!"

"It's OK," the girl said, stroking Pepper. "I like dogs." Pepper pushed her damp nose towards the girl's face. "And you're beautiful, aren't you?" she cooed, scratching Pepper behind the ears. Pepper wagged her tail and gave Ava a smug look.

Ava reached them and clipped Pepper's lead on. "Sorry," she apologized again as she caught sight of the muddy pawprints on the girl's jeans. "I do try to train her but she never listens."

The girl giggled. "It really is OK. I don't mind. What's her name?"

"She's Pepper and I'm Ava."

"I'm Lily," the girl said. "I live on Fentiman Road, just over there." She pointed across the main road.

"Same as me!" said Ava. "My mum and I have just moved into Curio House."

"That's the big house at the top of the street, isn't it?" Lily said.

Ava nodded and sat down beside her. With half-term and moving, it felt like ages since she'd actually talked to someone her own age. "What are you reading?" she asked.

Lily showed the book. "It's called *Magyck*."

So magic can be spelled like that, Ava realized,

thinking about the crystals.

Lily flashed her a shy smile. "I love reading," she carried on. "Particularly books about magic. I mean, I know magic isn't real of course," she added hastily, her cheeks going a little pink. "But wouldn't it be amazing if it was?"

"Yes!" said Ava. For a moment she considered telling Lily about the unusual crystals she'd found but decided it might sound too strange. "What school do you go to?" she asked instead.

"St Mary's," said Lily.

"That's where I'm going!" said Ava, pleased.

"What year?" Lily asked.

"Six," said Ava.

"Me too," said Lily, her brown eyes lighting up. "We'll be in the same class."

They smiled at each other.

"Lily! Time to go home!" the man on the bridge called.

Lily got to her feet. "I'd better go. I'll see you tomorrow at school."

"Yep, see you then," said Ava with another smile.

Lily gave Pepper a last stroke and then ran to join her parents and younger brother and sister. When she reached them, she waved shyly at Ava.

Ava waved back enthusiastically. "I've made a new friend," she told Pepper.

Pepper woofed.

"OK, we've *both* made a new friend," Ava said, stroking her.

She walked back to Curio House feeling happier and lighter than she had done in a while. It was great to have met someone her own age, particularly someone who seemed nice and would be at school with her. It made the thought of starting school the next day much more fun!

When Ava got home, she put the tomatoes and onions in the kitchen and headed to the Curio Room. She wanted to take another look at the crystals. Had she imagined the way they'd made her feel when she'd been holding them earlier?

She put a hand on the Curio Room door, but just then her mum came down the stairs. "How was your walk?"

"I met a girl who goes to St Mary's and is in the same class as me – she was really nice!"

Her mum smiled. "That's great, sweetie. And thanks for doing the shopping. Now, while I make dinner, can you go upstairs and get your school things ready for tomorrow?"

"OK," said Ava, reluctantly turning away. The crystals would have to wait.

She went up the wide staircase to her bedroom on the first floor. It was much bigger than her old room and had a bay window with a seat beside it. When she sat on it, she could watch the birds in the trees outside the window. Her mum had put up some new curtains and promised Ava she could choose how to decorate the room when they had a bit more money. For now, Ava had stuck some pictures she'd drawn of Pepper, and of people doing karate, on the walls with Blu-tack.

She packed her pencil case for the next day choosing her favourite pens, pencils and rubbers from the huge pile on her desk. There were even more art supplies piled up untidily on the shelves of her bookcase – Ava loved drawing and painting.

Once her pencil case was packed, she got out
her new school uniform. It was hanging next
to her white karate suit with its brown belt.
She couldn't wait for Mum to find her a new
karate club to go. She'd been doing karate since
she was seven and she really wanted to get her
black belt one day.

Ava put the grey school trousers and a red
polo shirt on her chair and then went to sit on
the window seat. Pepper jumped up beside her

32

and then flopped down, resting her chin on
Ava's knee. "I'm nervous about going to school,
tomorrow, Pepper," Ava murmured, stroking the
terrier's ears.

Pepper gazed up at her with soft, hazel eyes,
her ears flopping either side of Ava's knee. She
looked so cute that Ava leaned down and kissed
her nose. "But I think it will be fine," she said
optimistically. "At least I know Lily now."

"Ava! Supper!" her mum called.

Pepper knew that word! Leaping down from the window seat, she raced to the door and then woofed at Ava as if to say, *Hurry up, slowcoach!*

"OK, OK! I'm coming," Ava said, jumping up with a grin.

Ava and her mum had their own special tradition for the night before the first day of a new term. Ava's mum cooked spaghetti bolognese, which was Ava's favourite meal, and Ava chose a movie for them to watch – action adventure and funny movies were her favourite.

✦

At nine o'clock – tired, full and happy after watching her favourite film for about the twentieth time – Ava got into bed. She had to curl her legs up to avoid Pepper who was stretched out across the bottom of the bed in her favourite sleeping position – lying on her back with one front leg sticking up in the air as if she thought she was Superdog. Ava loved having

Pepper with her at night-time, although it did sometimes feel like the bed was more Pepper's than hers!

Shutting her eyes, Ava listened to the creaking of the house and the muffled clank of the hot-water system. Mum said all old houses made strange noises but Ava wasn't used to it yet and she still found the sounds hard to ignore. To distract herself she thought about the crystals. Surely she must have imagined the way they'd made her feel? *I must have done,* she thought. *I bet if I look at them tomorrow after school nothing will happen...*

An exciting thought crept into her head. *But what if something does?*

Eventually, Ava fell asleep, her dreams full of glittering crystals, but at some point in the middle of the night, a noise woke her up. She tried to go back to sleep but then she heard it again: a *thump thump* that sounded like it was coming from the staircase.

Thump. Pause. *Thump.*

Ava frowned. Was it her mum? It didn't sound like footsteps… It sounded like something jumping up the staircase one step at the time.

She heard a faint scrabbling noise on the floorboards outside her room. Pepper let out a low growl. Ava put her arms round her. "What is it, Pepper?" she whispered.

Pepper's body quivered as she growled again.

Ava hesitated and then made her mind up. She had to find out what was making the noise!

Getting out of bed, she tiptoed to the door.

Her heart pounded as ideas filled her head – ghosts, zombies, monsters…

None of those are real, Ava reminded herself firmly.

She opened the door and peered into the gloomy corridor. The scrabbling noise had stopped. She looked into the shadows and up the staircase that led to the second floor. There was absolutely nothing there.

Weird, she thought. Shutting her door, she hurried back to the warm bed. Pepper had settled down again, now curled up, her nose on her paws. Ava listened a bit more but there was no sound apart from the occasional gurgle of the pipes. She tucked her feet underneath Pepper and before she knew it, she had fallen asleep.

CHAPTER THREE

"Mum, did you hear anything in the night?" Ava asked at breakfast the next morning.

"I told you not to worry about the noises the house makes," her mum said. "Just think of it as the house talking to you and wanting you to feel at home."

"But this was a different sound. It wasn't the pipes, it was like something moving around, a kind of scrabbling," said Ava.

"I suppose it may have been mice," her mum said thoughtfully. "I haven't seen any sign of them but a mouse could have found its way inside when we were moving in. I'll have a look round later. Now, time to get a move on." She got to her feet. "You don't want to be late on the first day at your new school!"

✦

St Mary's was only three streets away from Curio House but Ava and her mum set off with plenty of time to spare. Ava couldn't help thinking about all her friends at her last school. She'd kept in touch with them and her mum had promised she could go back and visit but it wasn't the same as seeing them every day. Soon they'd be going into their old classroom, sitting down at their desks, chatting about the half-term holiday. Thinking about that made Ava start to feel sad so she quickly stopped. She needed to focus on her new school and making new friends.

I hope my teacher's nice, she thought. Her old

teacher had never made Ava feel bad for finding reading and spelling hard, and Ava's friends had also helped her. Her stomach twisted into knots as she and Mum got closer to her new school. What if it was different here?

Ava spotted Lily heading into the playground with a shorter girl with shoulder-length blond hair.

"That's the girl I met yesterday, Mum," she whispered. "Shall I go and say hi?"

"She looks nice but you'd better stay with me, sweetie," her mum said. "We need to go to the school reception."

They went in through the front door and spoke to the secretary, who told them her name was Lisa, and then they met the headteacher – Mrs Mistry.

Ava said goodbye to her mum in the reception area. "I'll wait in the playground for you after school," her mum told her. "Have a really good day."

"Thanks, Mum." Ava gave her a quick hug and then followed Lisa to the Year Six classroom.

To Ava's relief, the looks the other girls and boys in the classroom gave her as she walked in were curious but not unfriendly, and the teacher, Ms Haynes, welcomed her warmly. "Hi, Ava, come in."

"Ava! Hi!" Ava saw Lily at a nearby desk, sitting next to a boy with red hair. She was waving eagerly at her.

Ava waved back.

"Do you two know each other?" Ms Haynes asked.

"We met yesterday," Ava replied.

"Great! Lily can be your buddy. Why don't you go and sit next to her? Fin, you can move next to Oscar."

Fin, the boy with the red hair, smiled at Ava before moving his books so Ava could take his place.

"We start each morning with silent reading," Ms Haynes told Ava. "Lily will show you where the books are."

Lily took Ava to a bookcase at the back of the class. "You can choose anything you like."

Ava hesitated. Should she choose a thick book with lots of words, the kind Lily had been reading the day before? But she knew she'd never finish a book that long. Instead, she chose a book that had a cartoon dog on the cover and lots of pictures. She'd read a couple of books in the series before. She glanced at Lily, wondering what she thought of her choice and whether she'd say it was babyish, but to her relief, Lily didn't.

"I love those books!" Lily said. "I've got the whole series at home. Come on, let's sit back down."

Ava tried to read but as usual the letters seemed to jump around. *Left to right,* she reminded herself, using her finger to point to the words. Luckily there were so many cartoon pictures she didn't need to read all the words to work out the story. After a while, she took out a pencil and mini notebook, copied one of the drawings from the book and then added her own cartoon beside it.

"That's really good!" whispered Lily, looking over her shoulder. "I wish I could draw like that."

"Thanks, I love drawing," Ava whispered back, pleased.

After registration and morning assembly, their first lesson was maths. Ava whizzed through the questions and was able to help Lily when she got stuck. After maths they worked in pairs to make a poster about endangered animals. Lily was happy to write out notes while Ava drew the headings and pictures to illustrate it.

They chatted happily as they worked. Ava told Lily she liked drawing and karate, and Lily told Ava she liked animals and reading and writing stories.

"What kind of stories?" Ava asked.

"They usually have magic in," said Lily. "I want to be an author when I'm older."

"Do you draw pictures too?" Ava asked.

"No, I'm rubbish at drawing." Lily's eyes widened. "Maybe we could do a book together? I could write it and you could do the pictures."

Ava beamed. "Definitely! You could come

44

round to my house one day and we could make a start on it."

"I'd love that," said Lily. "I've always thought your house looks like something from a story book. The kind of house where mysteries happen."

Ava thought about the scrabbling noise she'd heard in the night and the strange box of crystals she'd found. "I know exactly what you mean," she agreed.

They swapped mobile phone numbers and agreed to ask their mums if they could meet up after school that week.

At breaktime they went outside together. The girl who Ava had seen Lily walking into school with came running over. "Hey, Lily!" She gave Ava a curious look.

"Hi, I'm Ava," Ava said.

"Ava's new here, Sarah," Lily explained. "She just started in Year Six. Ms Haynes has asked me to be her buddy."

"Oh." From the way Sarah started to bite her lip, Ava got the feeling that Sarah wasn't too pleased by the news.

"Sarah's in Year Five," Lily told Ava. "We're cousins."

"And best friends," said Sarah quickly, linking arms with Lily. "Should we go and sit on the wall?"

"OK. Are you coming?" Lily said to Ava.

Ava had the feeling Sarah didn't want her to tag along and she didn't want to cause problems. Also, though Lily was really nice, she wanted to get to know other people in her class too. "It's OK. You two go. I'm going to fill up my water bottle."

Lily looked disappointed but Sarah was clearly

46

relieved. "See you then, Ava. Come on, Lily," she said, dragging her cousin off.

Ava wandered away. A group of girls were sitting on a bench chatting but they were doing each other's hair and passing round lip gloss and she decided not to interrupt them. She wasn't that into sitting round and talking. She liked to be more active at breaktimes.

A few of the girls from her class were playing football with some of the boys. She watched as they charged up and down. Ava spotted the boy who had been sitting by Lily and smiled at him. Fin smiled back and called over to her. "Do you want to play, Ava?"

"Sure," said Ava and, putting her water bottle down, she ran to join in.

She had fun and by the end of break she had managed to learn the names of the people she was playing with. As well as Fin, she met Oscar, Jack, Millie, Safiya and Elenoor and they all seemed really friendly.

When she got back into the classroom, Lily was sitting at their desk. "I'm sorry about Sarah earlier," she said awkwardly. "She can be a bit shy with people she doesn't know."

"It's fine," said Ava, meaning it. "I had fun playing football."

Lily looked relieved she wasn't in a mood. "So shall we do some more on this poster then?"

Ava smiled. "Sounds good to me!"

The rest of the day flew by. At lunchtime, Lily hung around with Sarah, and Ava played football again.

"So how was your first day?" her mum asked when she collected her. "Did you make any friends?"

Ava nodded. "Everyone was really nice and I'm sitting next to Lily, that's the girl I met yesterday. She's over there." She pointed out Lily who was standing with Sarah and a man who looked like he might be Sarah's dad. Seeing Ava looking at her, Lily waved and made a *phone me* gesture.

Ava grinned and nodded. She definitely would.

✦

When Ava got home, she greeted Pepper with cuddles and kisses and then changed into warm clothes – jeans, hoodie and fluffy socks. The heating in the house wasn't very good and it always felt cold. On her way down the stairs, with Pepper bounding beside her, she paused. The stairs were wooden at the edges with faded carpet running up the middle, leaving a gap of dark wood on each side. There were some scratch marks on the wood that Ava couldn't remember seeing before. She might not be good at reading but she was very good at remembering what things looked like and spotting when anything had changed, and she was absolutely sure the scratch marks were new. She examined them. They looked like they had been made by small, clawed feet.

It could have been the mouse I heard last night, she thought. *Though it'd have to be a pretty big mouse to make marks as deep as that.* She looked at Pepper, who had run on and was now waiting at the bottom of the stairs. Could it have been Pepper? No, she'd been to the dog groomer's just before they moved and her claws had been trimmed then too.

Feeling puzzled, Ava continued downstairs to the Curio Room. The air had the same strange stillness as the day before and as she hurried over to the desk, she noticed that some of the curios had moved. The cat-headed figurine had fallen over, the metal goblet was lying on its side and the crocodile mummy was now on the floor. Ava frowned. Maybe her mum had been in the room, but surely she'd have picked the things up if she'd knocked them over?

Spotting the crocodile, Pepper trotted over to it, her ears pricking.

"Oh no, you don't," said Ava, swooping down to pick it up. She put it back on the same shelf she'd left it on the day before, feeling a flicker of guilt as she saw its torn and unravelling bandages. The creature's head was poking out more now, revealing dried leathery skin and tips of small, razor-sharp teeth just visible around its mouth. Its little clawed feet and the end of its tail were also sticking out of the bandages.

"Oh, Pepper," she said, shaking her head. "Great-Aunt Enid wanted us to look after these things. I don't think she would have been very pleased if she knew you'd chewed her Egyptian crocodile!"

She quickly set the figurine and cup the right way up and then picked up the black-and-white stone that she'd left next to the mummy, feeling a spider tingle of dread running down her spine.

She carried the stone to the box on the desk and shoved it into its compartment. Immediately, the horrible feeling left her. Ava swallowed. She'd convinced herself that she must have imagined the way the crystals had made her feel but suddenly she wasn't so sure.

She looked at the crystals, shining and glittering in their little compartments. It was an impossible idea but could they ... could they actually be magic like the words on the box said?

Ava pushed the thought away. No – magic was just pretend.

So why do they make me feel so strange? a little

voice in her head said.

Wondering if the handwritten notes on the inside of the box lid would give her more of an idea, Ava studied it, but the writing was very difficult to read. She felt like stamping in frustration as she tried to sound out the words.

A picture of Lily popped into her head. Lily was good at reading, and she had said she wished magic was real – perhaps Lily would help? But what if she hadn't been serious? What if she just laughed at her? What if she told everyone at school that Ava had a box of crystals that she thought were magic and then no one wanted to be friends with her?

Ava thought for a second and then made up her mind. If she wanted to find out more about the mysterious crystals, it was a risk she was going to have to take!

CHAPTER FOUR

Her mind made up, Ava ran upstairs to find her phone. She wasn't allowed to take it to school so had left it on her desk. She found Lily's number in her school bag and punched it in.

"Hello?" Lily answered cautiously.

"Hi. It's me – Ava!"

"Ava!" Ava heard the smile in Lily's voice. "I wasn't sure who it was. I haven't put your number into my phone yet."

Ava didn't want to waste time. "Do you want to come round?"

55

"What? Now?" said Lily, sounding surprised.

"Yeah. I've got something I really need some help with."

"Sure," said Lily. "I'll check with my mum. It'll only take me a few minutes to get to yours."

Ava felt a rush of relief. "Great! See you soon!"

She rang off and then went to find her mum. "I've just asked Lily round, is that OK?" Ava knew her mum would say yes. She was very relaxed about things like that.

"Of course, sweetie," her mum said. "It's lovely you've made a friend so quickly. Help yourselves to whatever snacks you want."

"Thanks, Mum!"

Ava ran to the hall to wait and a few minutes later, Lily arrived.

"Oh my gosh," she said, walking into the house and looking round at the high ceilings, the old paintings and the wide wooden staircase that led upstairs to the first floor. "This place is so old!"

"And cold," said Ava. "I'd keep your coat on if

I were you!" She shut the door as Lily crouched down to say hello to Pepper who was bouncing around her legs.

"So what do you want help with?" she asked, glancing up at Ava.

Ava decided it was easier to show her than explain. "Come with me."

Leaving her trainers and hat by the door, Lily followed Ava to the Curio Room.

"Look at all these things!" Lily breathed. She went over to the shelves and started reading the labels. "*Curse Cup. Nottingham. Circa 1505. Found in cellar of Lowdham Manor. Note the unusual carvings and code… Plaque with carving of Green Man. Cambridgeshire. Early 1100s. Note the vines for hair… Guardian Stone Gargoyle. Eastwold. Circa mid-1200s. Removed from church when it was renovated in 1810. Note open mouth to inspire fear in enemies…*" She looked at Ava. "How come these things are here and not in a museum?"

"They belonged to my mum's great-aunt
Enid." Ava explained about Great-Aunt Enid's
will and her mum inheriting the house.

"You're so lucky," said Lily enviously.

"Yes, because *everyone* wants to live in a house
filled with curse cups and old mummies!" said
Ava with a grin.

Lily giggled. "It's better than big spiders!
We've got lots in our house and I really hate
them. So is the reason you asked me here
something to do with these weird things?"

"Kind of." Ava showed her the crystals. "Don't laugh but there's something strange about the crystals in this box. On the lid it says they're magic crystals…"

"Magic?" Lily squeaked.

Ava nodded. "I don't know if they are for sure but when I touch them, they make me feel odd." She waited for Lily to laugh but Lily didn't. "There's some writing inside the box but… Well, I can't read it. I thought you might be able to and it might help me work out what the crystals are for." She looked at Lily hopefully.

Lily's eyes were glowing with excitement. "Oh, wow! This is amazing. Of course I'll help!"

Relief rushed through Ava. "Why don't you touch the crystals and see what happens to you?"

Lily slowly touched a blue crystal with one finger. Ava studied her expectantly. Lily waited a moment and then gave Ava a wary look. "Is this just a game?"

"No!" Ava insisted. "I promise it's not. Are

you not feeling anything?"

Lily shook her head.

"Try that one instead!" Ava pointed to the glossy green crystal with the purple stripe that she'd held the day before – the one that had made her feel strong, calm and clear-headed.

Lily read the label aloud: "*Fluorite.*"

"Well?" Ava said impatiently as Lily picked it up.

"I'm not feeling anything."

Ava felt a rush of disappointment but then…

"Hang on … wait." Lily shut her eyes. "Yes, I'm starting to feel … kind of peaceful. Like everything is good and there's nothing at all to worry about."

Delight flooded through Ava. "That's sort of how I felt too!"

A smile crossed Lily's face and she nodded, her eyes still shut. "Mmm," she murmured happily and then she yawned.

"Lily?" said Ava.

Lily didn't reply. Her head had started to sink to one side, as if she was falling asleep.

"Lily!" exclaimed Ava, grabbing her arm and shaking it.

Lily's eyes blinked open. "What? Oh my gosh! I felt so chilled I started falling asleep. I don't know why."

"It was the crystal!" said Ava excitedly. If the crystals made Lily feel things too then it meant there was definitely something strange about them.

Magic, a little voice in her mind whispered. *Just like the box says.*

"Try holding the dark grey crystal with red patches next," Ava suggested.

"*Bloodstone,*" Lily read out. After a few minutes of holding the red-and-grey crystal she started fidgeting, moving her hands and feet as if she couldn't keep still. "My body feels all tingly, like I've got to move."

"It made me leap into the air," said Ava.

"I also feel like nothing in the world could scare me. I could even hold a spider right now – a big one with hairy legs!" said Lily. She started to jog on the spot. "And, whoa! I … I can't keep still!"

"Put it down!" exclaimed Ava.

Lily hastily put the crystal down. "OK, that was very weird!"

"We need to find out more," said Ava. "Can you read the notes?"

Lily studied the inside of the lid, her eyes moving rapidly over the words. "It's a list of all the crystals. Listen to what it says about the crystal I was just holding. *Bloodstone: the Energy Crystal. Bloodstone increases energy and courage. It also enhances physical powers and decision-making.*" She looked up. "That must be why I felt like I couldn't stop moving!"

"And why you felt brave enough to suddenly want to cuddle a spider!" said Ava.

"There are notes on all the crystals," said Lily. "This is what it says about the first one I held. *Fluorite, the Calming Crystal. Fluorite grounds the mind, heightens intuition and eases stress and tension.*" Lily looked up. "Ava, it sounds like the crystals can make people feel different things."

It was what Ava had been suspecting but hearing it spoken aloud made it suddenly, wonderfully real. "This is so cool! What do the other crystals do?"

Lily pointed to each crystal in turn. "*Rose Quartz, the Peace Crystal. Aventurine, the Fortune Crystal. Amethyst, the Manifestation Crystal. Lapis Lazuli, the Truth Crystal; Tourmaline, the Protective Crystal; Dalmatian Jasper, the Restorative Crystal; Obsidian, the Seeing Crystal and Jade, the Dream Crystal.*

This is amazing! What are you going to do, Ava? Will you tell your mum?"

Ava shook her head. Her mum was great and Ava usually told her everything but she didn't want to risk her taking the crystals away. Not when there was still so much to discover! "Can it be our secret? At least for now."

"OK," Lily agreed eagerly.

"Let's see what happens when we touch the other crystals," said Ava. "How about that truth one?"

"Lapis Lazuli," said Lily, pointing to a beautiful deep blue crystal.

As Ava took it out of the box, she immediately felt a strange loosening sensation inside her, as if a knot had been undone.

"Well? How do you feel?" Lily demanded.

"I feel... I feel..." Suddenly it was as if Ava had lost control of her mouth. Words came tumbling out. "I feel really stupid when I try to read but I can't and when I write because my

spelling is so bad. I feel sad sometimes because
I don't see my dad very often and when I do
go and stay with him he's always busy with
baby Fergus and doesn't have time for me..."
She dropped the stone in shock and stared
at Lily, her cheeks flushing red. She couldn't
believe she'd just blurted out her deepest secrets
in front of someone she'd only just met.
What would Lily think?

There was a long moment of silence and
then to Ava's surprise, Lily suddenly picked up
the stone.

"I really wouldn't do that," said Ava quickly.

Lily ignored her and shut her eyes. "The magic's starting to happen."

"Are you OK?" Ava asked cautiously.

Lily's speech got faster. "I feel cross at times because I always have to be the responsible one. Huy and Mai have tantrums and it's always me who has to give way and give up what I want to do. I love them but sometimes I wish I didn't have a little brother and sister and I know that's really horrible but just for a second I feel it."

Ava suddenly realized that Lily had taken hold of the Truth Crystal so that Ava wouldn't be the only one who felt embarrassed. "Lily, you can put—"

Lily rushed on. "I feel fed up with Sarah at times too. She's my best friend and she's my cousin but she never lets me be friends with anyone else. She came back from living abroad last year and I thought she'd make lots of friends but she only seems to want to be friends with me…" Her cheeks turned bright red.

"Lily," Ava interrupted. "Put the stone down."

Lily dropped it back in the box. She stared at her hands.

"Thanks," said Ava quietly. "That was really nice of you."

Lily swallowed. "I … I don't think I like that stone very much."

"Me neither," said Ava. "Though it would be fun to try it out on the teachers at school. Imagine what *they'd* say!"

Lily smiled, her embarrassment fading. She looked at the crystals. "I wonder why that black-and-white stone is so much bigger."

"I touched it yesterday and it made me feel horrible," said Ava with a shudder.

Lily read the label beside the stone. "It's called the *Osiris Stone.* I think I saw something about it right at the end of all the writing."

Just then, Lily's mobile rang and she checked the screen. "It's my mum." She answered it. "OK… Yes… OK," she said into the phone.

Ending the call, she pulled a face at Ava. "I've got to go," she said. "Mum wants me home before it gets dark."

"Do you want to come round again tomorrow so we can find out more about the crystals?" Ava asked eagerly.

"Definitely!" said Lily

Ava felt her tummy fizz. This was the most exciting thing that had ever happened to her and it was brilliant to have a friend to share it with!

✦

Ava's mum insisted they walked Lily home. When they got to Lily's house, they all went inside and the two mums had a cup of tea while Lily showed Ava her bedroom. It had a bookcase full of books and there were more piled on the floor. Posters of cute animals covered the walls and she had fairy lights around her bed. Her little brother and sister, Huy and Mai, peeped shyly round the door at Ava.

"Hi," said Ava, waving at them.

Huy, who was two, hid behind Mai, but the little girl was bolder. "Will you play schools with me?" she asked.

Lily glanced at Ava who nodded and so they all played schools in Mai's room. It was fun, although Ava could see why Lily sometimes felt fed up with her little brother and sister. Little kids were very hard work! Lily, however, was very patient and constantly kept the peace. When Mai and Huy got bored of playing normal schools, Ava suggested they played karate school and taught them both some karate moves, which they loved!

"Thanks for helping me with them," Lily said when it was time for Ava to go.

"It's fine. Thank *you* for helping *me* earlier." They exchanged grins.

"Lily seems nice," said Ava's mum as she and Ava walked home.

Ava remembered the way that Lily had taken a turn with the Truth Crystal to make her feel better. "Yes, she really is," she agreed.

CHAPTER FIVE

That night, Ava woke to hear something
scrabbling outside her room again. *It's just a
mouse*, she reminded herself. But hearing thuds
on the staircase leading up to the second floor,
she sat up. "Pepper?" she said, poking the terrier
with her toes. "Can you hear that?"

Pepper opened one eye but then closed it
again and went straight back to sleep.

"Some guard dog you are!" Ava whispered.
There was another thud and curiosity got
the better of her. If it was a mouse then it

71

was a monster one!

Swinging her feet out of bed, Ava went to her door. She was just in time to see a shadowy shape with a long tail disappear up the top of the second set of stairs. It looked a lot larger than a mouse. Maybe it was a rat? Ava hastily shut her door. She didn't mind mice but she definitely didn't want a large rat running around in her bedroom!

Dashing back to bed, she pulled the duvet over her head and tried to ignore the scrabbling noises now coming from the landing above her head.

✦

Ava didn't sleep well for the rest of that night. Her dreams were full of huge rats and magic crystals. On her way downstairs the next morning, she looked for evidence of the rat but the only thing she saw were a few more scratches and some strange damp patches on the runner that carpeted the stairs. The damp patches continued all the way to the kitchen. Pushing open the door, she was surprised to see that Pepper's water and food bowls were both empty. Ava always put dry dog biscuits in Pepper's bowl in the evening in case Pepper was hungry but Pepper normally ignored them. She preferred to eat human food and would usually only eat dog biscuits if they had gravy on!

"Did you decide to have a midnight snack last night?" Ava said to Pepper. Then a thought struck her. "Or maybe the rat ate your biscuits!"

Pepper sniffed her empty bowl and then sat down, looking confused.

"Rat?" her mum echoed, coming into the kitchen. "What rat?"

73

"I saw a rat in the night. It went up the stairs to the top floor."

Ava's mum shuddered. "Ew! Mice aren't too bad but rats are a different matter." She shook her head. "Honestly, old houses! They have so many problems, not to mention all the dusting!"

"Did you dust the Curio Room yesterday?" Ava asked, remembering how some of the objects had been knocked over.

"No, I'm staying out of there for now and concentrating on the rooms we use most," said her mum. "Why?"

"Oh, no reason," said Ava, feeling puzzled. The shelf the objects had been on was too high for Pepper to reach, so if her mum hadn't knocked over the objects then who – or what – had?

+

It was really hard not talking to Lily about the crystals at school but the only times they could talk privately were at break and lunch, and then

Sarah stuck to Lily's side like glue so Ava ended up playing with other kids in her class instead.

At the end of school, Sarah ran up to Lily. "Are you ready to go?"

"Um." Lily looked awkward. "Sorry, Sarah, but I can't walk home with you tonight. I'm going to Ava's for tea."

"Oh." Sarah's face fell.

Ava felt torn. She hated upsetting people and although Sarah hadn't been very friendly towards her, Lily had said it was because Sarah was shy. She almost asked Sarah if she wanted to come with them but because of the crystals she kept quiet.

"Do you want to come round to mine for tea tomorrow?" Sarah asked Lily, not looking at Ava.

"Yes, of course," Lily said quickly.

Looking happier, Sarah ran to meet her dad.

"Should I invite her round to mine too?" Ava asked. She didn't like the thought of Sarah feeling left out.

Lily hesitated and then shook her head. "No, we wouldn't be able to find out more about the crystals if Sarah was there. She'd just laugh if we told her we thought the crystals could make us feel things. She's really into science and doesn't believe in magic at all. Don't worry," she said as Ava's eyes followed Sarah across the playground. "I'll go to hers tomorrow. She'll be fine!"

+

It started raining as they walked back to Ava's and when they got there, the house felt cold. They kept their coats on and fetched some biscuits to eat. Pepper was very excited to see them both, jumping up at them and trying to lick their faces.

"Pepper, I've only been away for a day!"

Ava laughed, crouching down to stroke her. "Have you missed me, you silly do—" She broke off as Pepper cheekily snatched the cookie from her hand. Darting away before Ava could grab her, she gobbled it up.

"Pepper!" Ava exclaimed.

Lily grinned. "She's so naughty."

"That was very sneaky!" Ava said, trying to sound stern. Pepper just wagged her tail, taking no notice at all of the telling-off.

Ava got herself another cookie and they went to the Curio Room. She frowned as she saw that all the figurines on one shelf had been knocked over, the jewellery was jumbled together in a heap and the crocodile mummy that had been on that shelf was nowhere to be seen - there was just a pile of dirty bandages lying on the floor nearby. Ava went over and poked them.

"What are you doing?" Lily asked.

"There should be a crocodile in these bandages," said Ava, holding them up.

"A what?"

"The mummified baby one," Ava said. "It was here yesterday." A horrible thought struck her as Pepper sniffed at the bandages in her hands. "Oh no. Pepper, you didn't eat it, did you?"

Pepper looked at her through her fringe and wagged her tail.

"How would Pepper have got on to the shelf?" said Lily. "It's too high for her to reach."

Ava frowned. "Maybe the mummy somehow fell off."

"I guess so," said Lily. "I mean, it can't have crawled out of those bandages by itself."

Ava grinned. "You never know, it could be a zombie crocodile mummy." She grabbed Lily's arm. "Watch out!" she said, pretending to be scared. "It could be waiting to pounce on us and eat our brains!"

"We need weapons!" said Lily, playing along and grabbing a fan made of ostrich feathers from the shelves. She held it out like a sword.

Ava giggled. "How exactly do you think you could defeat a zombie with a fan?"

"Um, I could tickle it to death?" said Lily.

They both snorted with laughter.

Lily put down the fan and then went over to the box of crystals that were still on the desk. She began to read the notes out as Ava hid the bandages under the shelf so her mum wouldn't see them if she came in. "*The magyck crystals contain ancient earth magic.* Oh wow! Magic!" she breathed.

"Keep reading," Ava urged.

Lily carried on. "*The crystals each have their own energy field and powers, which can be used by those with an open mind. Their powers will be magnified when they are placed in the amulet, surrounded by the three stones of clear quartz...*"

"What's the amulet?" interrupted Ava.

"I guess it's this," said Lily, taking the necklace out of the box and holding it up. The triangular pendant hanging from it had had three clear crystals, one in each point of the triangle and a round space in the centre with little clips that looked just the right size for the crystals in the box. Lily read on. "*Before being placed in the amulet, a crystal's magyck should be activated by someone connecting their energy to it...*"

"What does that mean?" interrupted Ava.

Lily shrugged. "I don't know." She continued to read. "*Once in the amulet, the person wearing it will be able to direct the magyck, but beware! If the amulet is used by someone with an unfocused mind, the magyck may behave unpredictably.*

When a crystal's magyck has been used up, it can be recharged by..." She broke off. "The next words are smudged."

"Never mind." Ava didn't want to spend more time reading. "I vote we put a crystal into the necklace and see what happens. How about this one?" She picked out a pretty purple stone. "What does it do?"

Lily read the label and checked the notes. "That's Amethyst. It's the Manifestation Crystal."

"What does that mean?" Ava asked, placing the stone in the centre of the pendant. There were three little clasps to hold it in place.

"I'm not sure," said Lily. "Let me see…" She broke off as the purple crystal started to glow. "Oh my … wow!" she squeaked as it got brighter and brighter, throwing purple light around the gloomy room. Pepper barked in alarm and backed away.

"It's proper magic!" breathed Ava. "Awesome!"

She put the necklace over her head and immediately felt as if she was sparkling too.

Pepper hid under the desk and whined.

"It's OK, Pepper," Ava reassured her. "Don't be scared. Come here." She reached into her coat pocket for some dog treats but the packet was empty. *I need to get some more.* The thought flashed through her mind and a moment later something hit her head. *What was that?* Ava looked up and saw some small brown objects the size of hazelnuts appearing out of thin air. They rained down gently.

"What's going on?" Lily asked faintly.

"I have absolutely no idea," said Ava, her eyes wide.

A pellet rolled towards Pepper. She gave it a sniff and gobbled it up.

"No, Pepper!" gasped Lily. "They could be poisonous."

Ava picked up a pellet from the floor. It looked very familiar. "They're not poisonous," she said, looking at Lily. "They're dog treats!"

CHAPTER SIX

Ava and Lily stared at each other in astonishment while Pepper woofed happily and started to hoover up the meaty snacks.

"It must be the crystal," said Lily, grabbing the box. "*Amethyst: the Manifestation Crystal. Amethyst makes that which is desired become real. It enhances intuition and clear thinking.*" She looked up. "Ava, what were you thinking about when the crystal started to glow?"

"That I needed some more dog treats... Oh!" Ava broke off as she realized what must have happened.

Lily had clearly realized the same thing. "The crystal made treats appear because you wanted them!"

"Seriously?" Ava said in dismay. "Why wasn't I thinking about chocolate? OK, OK, I'm thinking about chocolate now." She looked up hopefully but no chocolate appeared and the dog treats continued to patter down.

Just then they heard Ava's mum calling to them from the other side of the house. "Ava! Lily!"

Ava looked at Lily in horror. "We can't let Mum come in here and see what's going on. Just imagine the questions she'll ask!"

"What shall we do?" said Lily.

"Panic!" cried Ava.

Ava and Lily started shoving handfuls of treats into their coat pockets but the more they picked up, the more fell! Brown bones bounced down around them faster and faster, covering the floor in a thick carpet.

"Let's chuck them outside!" said Ava, heaving up one of the old-fashioned windows and starting to throw handfuls of treats into the bushes.

Lily ran to help.

"Ava?" They could hear Ava's mum in the hall, outside the room.

Ava pulled off the necklace, threw it on to the desk and sprinted to the door. "Hi, Mum," she said, her heart pounding as she opened it a crack.

Her mum gave her a curious look. "What are

you two doing in there?"

"Nothing," said Ava quickly. "Nothing at all."

Her mum's expression grew suspicious.

"I mean, nothing for you to worry about. We're just … just working on a project," Ava gabbled. "It's a secret project. Yes, we want to surprise you with it so you can't come in. It's a… It's a…" She remembered what Lily had said at school the first day they'd met. "It's a book! We're making a book together."

"Oh, I see." Her mum's face cleared. "Well, that sounds intriguing. I'll leave you to it then. What would you like for tea?"

"Anything, please," said Ava, feeling weak with relief. The sound of treats pattering down had stopped and the room behind her was silent again.

"I'll put some pizzas on then. Is that OK, Lily? Do you like pizza?"

Lily appeared beside Ava and poked her head out. "Yes, Ms Romano," she said quickly.

"Thanks, Ms Romano. I love pizza, Ms Romano."

"You're easy to please," Ava's mum said with a smile. "And please, just call me Fran."

Lily smiled and nodded and they watched as Ava's mum went down the hall and into the kitchen.

Ava shut the door with a sigh of relief. "That was close!" She noticed something. "The treats! They've stopped appearing."

"And the crystal's stopped glowing." Lily pointed to the desk.

Ava hurried over and put the necklace back on but the crystal didn't glitter and shine again.

88

"Does that mean we've used the magic up?" She couldn't believe she'd wasted such amazing magic on conjuring dog treats!

"I don't think it's gone forever," said Lily thoughtfully. "Remember what I read about how the crystals can be recharged. I think the magic might run out but it can come back."

"How?" asked Ava.

"The words were smudged so I couldn't read them," said Lily. "I can try to work them out but, Ava, the important thing right now is that the magic worked. It really worked!"

A smile lifted the corners of Ava's mouth as Lily's words sank in. Her mum might have almost caught them and they had a lot more dog treats than Pepper could ever eat but the important thing – the amazing thing – was that the crystals actually *were* magic!

"You made dog treats appear from thin air!" Lily said, her eyes shining.

Excitement swept through Ava. "This is

incredible! We're going to have so much fun!"

Lily looked round. "First we need to do something about all these treats. We can't let your mum find them."

Ava scooped up a handful and went to the open window. "Let's throw them out here with the others. The bushes are so overgrown Mum won't notice and it might even make the rat go outside."

"Rat?" echoed Lily.

"I saw one last night, going upstairs," said Ava with a shudder. "It was massive and I think it ate Pepper's food and made scratch marks on the stairs. Let's leave the window open – if it smells the treats it might leave."

"Good thinking!" said Lily, hurrying to help her.

+

That night, Ava's mind was so busy turning over everything that had happened she couldn't get

to sleep. There was so much she wanted
to know! For a start, how could they recharge
the amethyst and make something more
interesting than dog treats appear? And why did
the crystals seem to work differently for her and
Lily? She'd noticed that when Lily had held the
Fluorite and Bloodstone crystals the day before
it had taken her longer to feel something and she
hadn't had quite the same reactions as Ava had.

The other thing she kept thinking about
was the words on the lid of the box: *Magyck
Crystals for…*

The faded words that followed those first three words were bugging her. For *what*? Did the crystals have a specific purpose then?

If they do, I'll find it out, she vowed as she finally fell asleep.

CHAPTER
SEVEN

Exhausted from all the excitement of the
evening before, Ava slept until her alarm went
off. On the way downstairs she checked the
carpet but there were no new scratch marks and
the carpet was dry. Pepper ran ahead into the
kitchen but Ava took a detour into the Curio
Room. She wondered if her plan had worked
and if the treats had tempted the rat outside.

A cold breeze was blowing in through the
open window. Ava went to shut it but as she
looked out, she frowned. All the treats in the

bushes had gone – every single one!

That's not possible, she thought in astonishment. *There were enough treats to feed a hundred rats! How come there's not one left?*

Hearing her mum call her, Ava pulled the window shut and noticed a few wet patches and muddy marks on the windowsill. However, she didn't have time to look at them properly. "Coming!" she shouted as her mum called her name again. Still feeling puzzled about the vanishing treats, she hurried out of the room.

When Ava arrived at school that morning, she found the playground was buzzing with strange news.

"All our fish have been stolen!" Fin was saying. "When Dad went into the garden this morning he saw puddles on the lawn and went to check the pond and realized the fish had gone!"

"Ours have disappeared too!" said Lily.

"And my grandad's. He lives near you," Elenoor said to Lily.

"Who'd want to steal fish?" said Safiya.

Jack grinned and put on a spooky voice. "Woooooo! It's the Fish Fiend of Fentiman Road!"

"I'm sorry about your fish," said Ava as she and Lily sat down in class.

"Thanks," she said. "I know you can't cuddle fish but I did really like them. I wonder who took them. It's so weird!"

"Very," Ava agreed.

Lily lowered her voice. "I wish I could come round to yours again tonight."

"Me too," whispered Ava. "I promise I won't do anything with the crystals without you, though. I thought I'd look through the desk and see if Great-Aunt Enid left anything useful about them. Remember how I told you she said in her will that the curios were special?" Lily nodded. "I bet she was talking about the crystals and that she knew they were magic!"

"Text me if you find anything interesting," Lily said.

"I will," promised Ava.

+

At the end of school, Lily came running over to Ava and her mum. "Sarah has an extra flute lesson tonight that she'd forgotten about so I can't stay at hers for tea after all. Could I come round to yours when she has to leave?"

"Oh yes, that would be great!" said Ava

in delight.

"You can have tea at ours if you like?" her mum added. "Then we'll walk you home."

"Thank you!" Lily said.

"We can keep working on our book," Ava said, winking at her.

Lily grinned and then glanced over her shoulder to where Sarah was watching them. "I'd better go. See you later."

+

When Ava and her mum got home, Ava took Pepper for a run outside. Pepper seemed very interested in sniffing the bushes and Ava had to use some of the dog treats that were still in her coat pocket to tempt her away.

"I bought some new dog chews," Ava's mum said when they arrived back in the kitchen. "Do you want to see if she likes them? They're on the side." She nodded to a plastic pot of dog chews on the counter.

Ava got some out. Pepper sniffed them for a moment, then carried them to her dog bed. She didn't chew them though, she just started to bury them under her blanket.

Ava's mum shook her head. "Sometimes I don't know why I bother."

Ava grinned. "Princess Pepper only likes human food and her treats - you know that, Mum!"

Leaving Pepper to bury her chews, Ava went through to the Curio Room.

The first thing she noticed as she pushed open the door was a strange, fishy smell in the room. She pulled a face. Maybe there were still some treats left and it was coming from them? Going to the window, Ava pulled it open to let some fresh air in.

As she did so, she noticed the muddy marks

she'd seen that morning on the window ledge. She studied them, mystified. They were dry now and they looked almost like paw prints but longer and pointier. Could Pepper have made them? But the terrier hadn't ever been in the room with muddy paws and, looking at the way they were pointing, they seemed to have been made by an animal coming *into* the room, not going out of it. Ava's scalp prickled and she glanced around. Could a wild animal have come in during the night? But the room looked just the same as always.

Ava went over to the desk. It was so tempting to try to do some magic with the crystals but she'd promised Lily she wouldn't use them without her, so instead she started to pull open the desk drawers, looking to see if Great-Aunt Enid had left any notes.

The door creaked. She turned round sharply but it was just Pepper, pushing it open with her nose. Ava resumed her search.

Most of the drawers were empty or just had pens and pencils in but in the last one she found a book on gods and goddesses from all different cultures.

Ava opened it curiously. The pages fell open at a page about an Egyptian god with a green

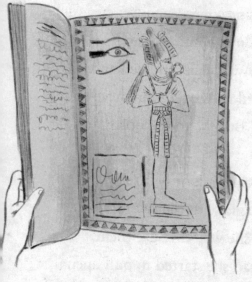

face who was holding something that looked like a shepherd's crook. The word under the picture caught her eye: *Osiris.* Ava frowned. *Where do I know that word from?*

She started to read what it said under the picture. "God of life, death, farming and..." she struggled to work out the final word, "res ... res-urr-ec ... resurrection!"

Ava broke off as Pepper started barking.

"What is it?" she said. Pepper was standing near the window, jumping backwards and forwards, barking at one of the long, heavy curtains. Remembering the strange marks by the window, Ava approached warily. Could it be a rat? A family of rats? Pepper's barks grew higher pitched as Ava got closer to the curtain. "It's OK, Pepper," she soothed.

Steeling herself, Ava grabbed the heavy material and pulled it to one side.

Her breath came out in a relieved rush as she saw a dark, leathery shape. It was just the crocodile mummy! Pepper hadn't eaten it after all! Though how it could have ended up behind the curtain and without its bandages she had no idea!

"Pepper! Be quiet! You've seen the mummy before." But as she moved to pick it up, Pepper's barking got even more frantic and she ran between the mummy and Ava.

"No, Pepper!" said Ava, thinking she was

going to snatch the mummy. She grabbed the
terrier's collar and, holding her back, reached for
the crocodile. But suddenly she paused, noticing
something. The mummy looked bigger than
before – longer and wider. And something else
was different too. Its lips were now curling back
from its razor-sharp teeth, there was mud on its
feet and a couple of thin, silvery discs caught
on its lips. Ava peered at it more closely. They
looked like … like fish scales.

Ava drew back as she remembered how everyone at school had been talking about how their fish had disappeared. *Could the mummy have had something to do with that…?*

No! She stopped herself there. That was ridiculous. The mummy was dead, not to mention a couple of thousand years old. How could it possibly have got out of the room?

Its feet do look muddy, though, she thought uneasily.

"Ava!" her mum shouted, interrupting her thoughts. "Dad's on the phone. He wants a chat."

Picking Pepper up, Ava backed away from the mummy. She knew it was odd but she suddenly felt like she didn't want to turn her back on it. Grabbing the crystals from the desk, she darted out of the room and slammed the door behind her.

CHAPTER EIGHT

"Oh, Pepper, you're gorgeous, yes, you're so beautiful," Lily cooed as Pepper jumped around her when she arrived at Curio House a little later. The terrier stood on her back legs, putting her front paws on Lily's knees. As Lily stroked her, she glanced at Ava. "You're quiet. Are you OK?"

"Yes… No… I don't know." Ava pushed a hand through her hair. She'd been waiting in the hall, willing Lily to arrive. She was desperate to talk to her about the crocodile.

Lily gave her a puzzled look and, managing to untangle herself from Pepper, she straightened. "What's up?"

"Let's go to my room," Ava said.

Looking very curious, Lily followed her upstairs.

Ava shut her bedroom door and they sat down on Ava's bed with the crystals between them. "OK, I know this sounds impossible," Ava began. "But I … I think that the crocodile mummy might have come back to life and eaten everyone's fish."

Lily's eyebrows flew up so high they hit her hairline. "What?"

"When I got home from school I found it behind the curtains without its bandages," Ava said quickly. "It's got mud on its feet, its mouth has changed and there are

105

things around its teeth that look like fish scales."

"But, Ava," Lily said, "it's a mummy!"

"I know," said Ava. "But I think it's been moving around."

"That's not possible," said Lily. "Mummies can't just resurrect themselves."

Ava squeaked. "What did you just say?"

"That it's not possible?" Lily said, puzzled.

"No, the resurrect bit! Resurrection means coming back to life, doesn't it?"

Lily nodded.

Ava remembered the book she'd found in Great-Aunt Enid's desk and her thoughts raced. "Osiris was the god of life, death and *resurrection*!" she said, pointing wildly at the box of crystals. "The Osiris Stone, Lily! The big black-and-white stone! Don't you see?"

Lily looked utterly confused. "I have no idea what you're talking about!"

Ava opened the box. "What if the Osiris Stone is like the god Osiris and has powers to bring things to life – to resurrect them – and now it's resurrected the crocodile!"

Lily grabbed the box. "I saw something about the Osiris Stone right at the bottom of the notes. I didn't read it because the writing was so small." Her eyes flickered over the notes on the lid and after a few moments, she drew in a sharp breath. "Oh."

"What?" asked Ava in alarm, seeing the horrified look on Lily's face.

Voice shaking, Lily read out, "*The Osiris Stone does not need the amulet to have its power magnified and it should be treated with great caution. One touch can kindle or snuff out a spark of life in a curio or other magical artefact. Darkness and light; life and death; two powers in one stone. To rekindle life, the light side of the stone must touch the artefact. The artefact will then achieve a temporary resurrection for twelve hours before returning to a deep sleep for a further twelve hours. With each day that passes the artefact will need less sleep and will become stronger and stronger until the resurrection is finally complete.*"

"This is not good," Ava whispered as the words sank in. "Not good at all. The Osiris Stone must have brought the mummy back to life."

"But the stone hasn't touched the mummy," Lily pointed out. "It's been in the box."

Ava licked her dry lips. "Not the whole time. The first day I found the crystals I took the Osiris Stone out. I put it and the crocodile mummy on the shelf together. It was that night that I heard a strange noise. The next night Pepper's food was eaten and her water was drunk. I don't think it was a rat after all, it was the crocodile coming back to life and exploring the house..."

"And last night we left the window open, so it could have got out and eaten everyone's fish!" Lily breathed.

Ava nodded. "It must have returned to the Curio Room each morning so that it could sleep close to the Osiris Stone."

"*With each day that passes the artefact will need less sleep and will become stronger and stronger.*" Lily gulped. "Ava, when exactly did you first leave the stone with the mummy?"

Ava's heart plummeted. "Three days ago." She jumped up. "Come on!"

They raced downstairs and opened the
Curio Room door. Ava's eyes flew to the place
where she'd last seen the crocodile mummy.
"Oh pants!" she whispered.

"What?" said Lily.

Ava gulped and pointed to the open window.
"It's gone!"

CHAPTER NINE

"There's a resurrected crocodile on the loose!" Lily gave Ava a horrified look.

"We need to catch it," said Ava, heading for the door. "It's hopefully not big enough to hurt a human yet but it could eat a cat or small dog. And if people find out about it there's no way we'll be able to keep the crystals secret any more!" She held up the box of crystals. "We should bring these. I've got a feeling we might need to use their magic."

Lily ran into the hall and grabbed her school

bag. "I can carry them in this."

Ava handed them over. "Mum, we're just taking Pepper for a walk!" she called. "Back soon!"

I hope, she added under her breath.

Ava grabbed Pepper's lead and clipped it on. If there was a hungry crocodile around she definitely wanted to keep Pepper where she could see her!

She and Lily hurried outside. Looking around

the overgrown garden, Ava spotted some tracks.
"Over there!" The marks, left by four clawed
feet in the damp grass, led to the gate.

"The crocodile's gone into the street!" said
Lily in dismay.

Running through the gates, they caught
their breath. Wheelie bins had been knocked
over and rubbish littered the pavement. Two
older men – one bald and one with a beard –
were looking at the mess.

"I can't believe it!" the bald one was saying. "What's happened here?"

"Teenagers," said the other man darkly. "You mark my words. Always messing around, causing trouble. They think this kind of thing's funny."

A grey-haired woman looked over a gate. "It wasn't teenagers, it was an animal. I saw it through my kitchen window. A strange-looking creature it was." She shook her head. "My eyes aren't what they used to be but it looked almost like a—"

"A dog," Ava exclaimed quickly, interrupting her. "I saw it in my garden too. It was definitely a dog."

Lily nodded hard. "Most definitely!"

"Dog owners," the grey-haired man sniffed. "Shouldn't have dogs if they can't control them."

"Ava, look!" whispered Lily, pointing to a broken garden fence.

They hurried over. The garden had a water

feature in. There were great puddles on the grass as if something had leaped through the water. Ava peered around warily. Was the crocodile still there? But no, she saw wet footprints further down the garden leading out through an open gate and on to the street.

"There it is!" gasped Lily as a long, thin shape darted out from behind a tree.

Pepper started to bark wildly. The crocodile mummy scuttled along the pavement, moving incredibly fast.

A cyclist turned up the road and the mummy shot out in front of the bike. The cyclist yelled in shock and almost fell off. "Did you see that?" he exclaimed as the crocodile disappeared under a parked car. "What on earth was it?"

"Just a dog," gasped Ava. "A very, very naughty dog!"

"Don't worry. We'll catch it!" said Lily.

The crocodile raced out from under the car and charged at three pigeons pecking near the corner shop.

Squawking in alarm the pigeons flapped into the air. The crocodile scuttled on to the main road. There was a loud squeal of tyres as drivers slammed on their brakes to avoid it.

Lily and Ava charged after it. Reaching the end of the street, they almost bumped into Sarah, who was cycling home from her flute lesson.

"You didn't tell me you were going to Ava's house," she said to Lily, looking hurt.

"Didn't I? Sorry!" gabbled Lily.

"We haven't got time to talk, Sarah," said Ava, her eyes scanning the riverbank across the road. "Come on, Lily. It may be by the river or even *in* the river!"

"What are you talking about?" said Sarah.

"Nothing, it's just... Just a game we're playing," Lily made up. "A kind of treasure hunt."

"Cool," said Sarah. "Can I join in?"

"No!" Ava and Lily said together.

Sarah frowned. "Fine, be like that." She got on her bike and rode off.

"I feel really mean!" Lily said to Ava.

Ava felt bad too but right now there wasn't time to do anything about it. They had a crocodile to catch! She saw Sarah stop a little way down the road and look back at them. "We can apologize tomorrow. Come on."

Checking the road was clear, they crossed it.

"Which way do you think it went?" said Ava, looking anxiously from side to side. To the right was town and to the left was countryside. Luckily the cold, wet weather seemed to be keeping most people inside but there was a group of teenage girls by one of the benches. Three of the girls were laughing, one was looking cross. "I'm not messing!" she said. "I just saw an alligator! It went into the water."

"What? To join its friend the Loch Ness monster?" said one of her friends with a grin.

"We're never going to believe you, Ellie," said another. "You might as well stop lying."

"I'm not lying," insisted Ellie. "It went that way." She pointed down the river, away from town.

Ava and Lily started running along the riverbank.

"Hey, don't go there, you two!" Ellie shouted. "There's an escaped alligator on the loose!"

Her friends burst out laughing and pulled her away.

Ava's breath came in short gasps as she ran along the path. Despite the cold, she was feeling very hot from running and her hair was sticking to her face. Were they ever going to catch up with the crocodile? What would happen if they didn't? Her stomach somersaulted at the thought.

The tarmacked path became a muddy track and entered a tunnel of trees. Thick reeds lined the riverbank and the air was heavy with the smell of damp vegetation.

"I can't run any more, Ava," panted Lily.

They slowed to a walk, drawing in great gulps of air. Ava heard a crack of a twig behind them and swung round. There was nothing there.

Just then, Pepper ran to the end of her lead and stood on the riverbank, barking. The reeds rustled and Lily squeaked. "Ava!"

Ava felt a rush of fear as the crocodile prowled out of the reeds, its eyes glittering with life. It was still a very dark brown colour and looked ancient but it was now even bigger, about a metre long. She guessed that the stone had made it bigger and stronger, and the river water had caused its dried-out body to fill out. Pepper barked hysterically, leaping at it and then jumping back as if she wasn't too sure what to do.

The crocodile didn't seem to have any doubts. Its beady eyes fixed menacingly on Pepper and it started stalking towards her, its jaws opening...

CHAPTER TEN

"No!" The yell tore from Ava as she sprinted forwards.

She flung herself down and pulled Pepper out of the way just as the crocodile's teeth snapped shut. Ava crashed to the ground with Pepper wriggling in her arms.

"Ava!" shrieked Lily as the crocodile started advancing on them both.

Ava's heart beat wildly as she stared up at the creature.

"Leave them alone, you creepy croc!" shouted

Lily. Picking up a fallen stick from the ground, she ran at the crocodile and poked it with the stick. The crocodile looked from one girl to the other, as if trying to decide who to attack first.

"Lily, get back!" shouted Ava desperately, struggling to her feet.

"No way!" Lily cried. "I'm not going to let you and Pepper get eaten by a crocodile! I'll defend you!" She waved the stick from side to side. "Get back, croc! I'm warning you!"

The crocodile caught the stick in its jaws and there was a crunch as it snapped it in two. Lily looked down at the little piece left in her hand. "Oh," she gulped.

The crocodile spat the rest of the stick out and lowered its head as if it was about to charge…

Suddenly, a high-pitched noise shrieked through the air. The crocodile recoiled. Still hanging on to Pepper who was barking and growling, Ava looked round and saw Sarah. She was standing by her bike, blowing her flute. The crocodile backed away into the reeds, shaking its head as if the sound was hurting its ears. They heard a splash as it entered the water.

Sarah lowered the flute. "OK," she said. "Is someone going to tell me what's going on?"

"You just saved us from a resurrected crocodile from Ancient Egypt!" Ava gasped.

"I did what?" Sarah's eyes widened like saucers.

Ava realized that they had to tell her the whole truth so – with Lily chipping in and Pepper bouncing around in excited circles – she explained about the crystals and the Osiris Stone bringing the crocodile mummy back to life. To Ava's astonishment, Sarah seemed to accept it all remarkably well.

"So you're trying to catch it?" she said.

"Yeah, though it might not have looked like that just now," said Ava ruefully.

"How did you know that your flute would scare it off, Sarah?" asked Lily.

"I know crocodiles have very sensitive hearing," Sarah replied. "When I saw it I thought blowing the highest note I could might make it back off – and luckily it did." She shook her head. "This is incredible. A mummified crocodile that's come back to life and magic crystals... Wow!"

"So you believe us?" asked Ava.

"I can't not, can I?" Sarah nodded at the river. "I just saw the evidence with my own eyes. What's the plan then? How are you going to change it back into a mummy?"

"Um…" Ava glanced at Lily who gave her a look that said she didn't have a clue. "We're not entirely sure," she admitted.

Sarah looked thoughtful. "What about the stone that brought it back to life in the first place? Could that change it back?"

Ava considered it. "The book said Osiris was the god of life *and* death. Can you read the notes again, Lily?"

Lily pulled the box out of her bag and read: "*The Osiris Stone must be used with great caution. One touch can kindle or snuff out a spark of life in a curio or other magical artefact. Darkness and light; life and death; two powers in one stone…"*

"*Two* powers in one stone!" interrupted Ava. "You were right, Sarah! I bet the stone can also be used to change the crocodile back into a mummy again. Come on!" She jogged off down the path.

"Wait, Ava!" Lily shouted. "How do you think you're going to get close enough to it to use the stone?"

Ava paused.

"You need to have a plan," said Sarah firmly. "You need to think of a way to attract it, then you need to work out how to make sure it can't hurt you."

Ava had an idea. "Pepper's lead! I'll tie it up with that!"

"How?" said Lily.

"I think I might know," said Sarah. "But we need something the crocodile likes to eat."

"Um … us?" said Ava.

"No!" Lily and Sarah said together.

126

Ava patted her pockets, trying to find something else. "Dog treats!" she gasped, pulling out a handful. Her pockets were still full of them from the other day.

"I've got loads too," said Lily.

"Great, then the only other thing we need is a phone," said Sarah.

"A phone!" spluttered Ava. "What are you going to do? Give it a call?"

Sarah ignored the question. "Listen, this is what we should do…"

CHAPTER ELEVEN

Ten minutes later, the girls and Pepper were crouching behind some trees further along the riverbank. Sarah had rung her dad. She told him she'd bumped into Lily and that she would be back later than expected, so not to worry.

She'd then used her phone to find a recording of a male crocodile trying to attract a mate. "We're going to play the recording to get the crocodile's attention," she explained. "It'll hear what it thinks is a handsome male crocodile and come swimming this way."

Ava was impressed. "How do you know so much about crocodiles?"

"We lived in Australia until a year ago," Sarah replied. "I learned about them there. I love learning about animals…"

"You love learning about everything," said Lily with a grin.

"True," said Sarah, grinning back.

"Wait a minute," said Ava, spotting a flaw in the plan. "How do we know our crocodile will appear when it hears the recording? We don't know if ours is a girl or a boy."

"It shouldn't matter," said Sarah. "Male crocodiles like to fight their rivals so even if ours is male, it should still want to investigate the noise. What we're going to do is lay a trail of dog treats from the river up to the trees and then, when it's eating, we'll all jump out from behind these bushes and grab it. It's not that big, so hopefully with three of us we'll be able to hold it still for long enough to wrap the dog lead around its jaws and stop it biting us…"

"Then we touch it with the Osiris Stone," said Ava, opening the box and looking at the big black-and-white stone. "And *ka-boom*! It turns back into a mummy. I'll do that bit. The crystals seem to work quickest for me." She ran her hand over them. One seemed to tingle under her fingers. Lifting her hand, Ava saw it was a pale green stone. "What's this one called?" she said curiously.

"Aventurine," said Lily, reading the label.

"What does it do?"

Lily read the notes. "*Aventurine brings luck, prosperity and good fortune, it also enhances leadership qualities.*"

"So it's a good luck crystal," said Ava slowly. Picking it up, she felt a current of energy run through her. Suddenly she felt taller, older and as if it was up to her to tell the others what to do. She also felt certain she needed to use this stone to stop the crocodile. "I'm going to put this in the necklace and wear it," she declared, taking the necklace out of the box.

"Why?" asked Sarah.

"I don't know," Ava said. "I just feel like it wants me to use it, so I'm going to."

Sarah frowned. "A stone can't want something."

"These crystals can." Ava saw Sarah open her mouth to argue and held up her hand. "No," she said firmly. "I know they're not living things like we are but they have their own energy and something is telling me we have to use this crystal if we want to catch the crocodile." She saw the surprise on Sarah's face and realized how bossy she had just sounded. The crystal was definitely affecting her. "I mean, please can we do it?" she added quickly.

"Of course we can," said Lily. She turned to her cousin. "Sarah, it might not make sense but Ava has a strong connection with the crystals. She can feel their powers much more quickly than I can. If she wants to use one of the crystals then I vote she should."

Sarah hesitated then shrugged. "Sure, if that crystal can bring us good luck then let's use it. The important thing now is catching the crocodile."

"You said it!" Ava slipped the stone into the centre of the pendant and grinned. "Come on, guys. It's time for us to croc 'n' roll!"

The green stone started to sparkle. Ava put the necklace over her head and every cell in her body tingled. She picked up the Osiris Stone and was relieved to find that with the Aventurine glowing, she didn't feel the same sense of dread as she had done when she'd held it before.

I can do this, she thought

confidently. *I can turn that crocodile back to a mummy!*

"Let's set our trail of treats," she said.

Sarah was fiddling with her phone. "I'll help you in a sec. There's something I need to do."

"Why don't you hold Pepper and I'll put the treats down?" Ava said to Lily. She pointed at the glittering crystal. "With this bringing me good luck I'm more likely to stay safe than you. In fact…" Ava trailed off. She had a feeling that the others wouldn't like the idea she'd just had at all!

She set a trail from the reeds up to the trees. When she'd finished, they all hid behind the bushes with Ava just about managing to stop herself from telling the others exactly where to sit and what to do.

Sarah turned the volume on the phone up, pressed *play* and a raucous cry rang out. None of them dared to speak. Would it work?

Sarah pressed *play* again to restart the video.

As the sound faded for a second time, they heard a splash. Pepper growled as a long brown snout poked out of the reeds and then a flat head emerged. Predatory eyes flickered from side to side, as the crocodile searched for the other crocodile it could hear. Hissing, it stomped out of the water and then its nostrils picked up the scent of the treats. It started to follow the trail towards the trees, snapping the treats up as it went.

"This is it!" Ava whispered, glancing at

her friends.

Lily was pale and looked terrified. Sarah was staring intently, watching the crocodile get closer. "OK," she breathed. "On the count of three. One…" Ava raced towards the crocodile.

"Ava! Wait!" Lily cried.

"What are you doing?" shouted Sarah.

Ava didn't stop. She was in command and she felt invincible! Leaping over a tree root, she landed in front of the crocodile. It lunged at her but she used one of the moves she'd learned in karate, kicking sideways with her foot and catching the side of its head.

It lurched to one side.

Go, me! Ava thought, giving a triumphant thumbs up to the others. Then, seeing a tree stump perfectly positioned beside the crocodile, she jumped on to it and sprang on top of the crocodile's body. She landed perfectly, pinning it down and holding on to the back of its head so it couldn't bite her.

The crocodile thrashed from side to side trying to throw her off.

"Oh no, you don't, Mr Snappy!" Ava cried. She'd never felt so cool!

Pulling the Osiris Stone from her pocket, she reached to touch the dark side to the crocodile but as she did so, the crocodile bucked violently. Ava lost her grip on the stone and it flew through the air, landing in the mud. The crocodile bucked again and this time she was flung off.

"Ava!" the others shrieked as she landed on her back.

Ava struggled to push herself up, her thoughts all over the place. What had just happened? She was supposed to have good luck! Glancing down at the crystal, she saw that it had stopped glowing – its magic had run out!

CHAPTER TWELVE

The crocodile stalked towards Ava. Lily and
Pepper charged forward, Lily yelling and
Pepper barking. The crocodile's attention barely
flickered in their direction. But then a noise
rang out – a deep, bellowing, booming sound
– that made it stop in its tracks. The crocodile
lifted its head.

Ava saw her chance. Scrambling across the
ground to the Osiris Stone, she grabbed it then
flung herself at the crocodile, touching the stone
to its back and holding it there.

For one terrifying moment, the crocodile's head swung towards her, its jaws opening, its knife-like teeth coming towards her, but then the stone's magic worked! The life died in the crocodile's eyes, its skin dried and hardened until it looked like old leather again and 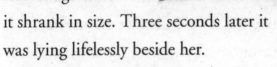 it shrank in size. Three seconds later it was lying lifelessly beside her.

Ava flopped back against the mud, too shocked to speak.

The next moment, Lily was flinging herself down beside her, and Pepper was licking her face. "Ava, are you OK?"

"Y-yes," said Ava shakily. "Though I almost wasn't. Of all the times for the magic to run out!" She sat up. "What was that noise?"

Sarah waved the phone at her as she came jogging over. "My back-up plan." She stopped next to them. "You should always have a Plan B in case Plan A goes wrong, so while you were putting the biscuits out I found another sound I know crocodiles react to, in case the mating call didn't bring it out of the river."

"It sounded like an angry hippo," said Ava.

Sarah grinned. "That's because it was! Crocodiles and hippos hate each other, so I thought the sound of one might work. It certainly worked as a distraction anyway."

"You're awesome," said Ava, shaking her head. "Thanks."

Sarah grinned. "No worries. You're pretty amazing yourself. Whatever made you decide to go all Karate Kid on the crocodile? That was so cool!"

"I thought that because I had the good luck stone, I wouldn't get hurt," said Ava. "Which was fine until the magic ran out."

She lifted the amulet. "We really have to work out how to recharge the crystals."

"We definitely do," agreed Lily. "But first we need to take the mummy back to your house where it belongs."

"Agreed," said Ava. She picked the crocodile up. "Come on, Mr Snappy. It's time to go home."

+

Sarah could hardly believe it when she walked inside the Curio Room. "Wow, this room is … well, it's…"

"Great!" said Lily enthusiastically.

"Kind of creepy?" suggested Ava.

"Definitely weird," said Sarah, going over to the shelves. "So your great-aunt collected all these things, Ava?"

"Yes, she said they were special and she wanted them to be kept together in this house after she died."

Sarah looked thoughtful. "I wonder why that was so important to her?"

Ava shrugged as she put the mummy at the back of the shelf and rearranged a few of the other curios. "Great-Aunt Enid was pretty unusual. I only met her once. She didn't really like having visitors."

"If you had a collection of cool things, I would have thought you'd want to show them off to people," said Lily.

"Unless there was a reason for keeping them secret." Sarah frowned. "Lily, can I see the crystal box? I noticed something on the lid earlier."

Lily handed the box over.

Sarah studied the outside. "What do you think these faded words say? *Magyck Crystals for...* Have you got paper and a pencil, Ava?"

Ava fetched some from the desk drawer and watched curiously as Sarah put the paper over the words on the lid and shaded over the top with the pencil. "What are you doing?"

"The words were stamped into the leather. By shading over the faded ones, we should be able to read them," Sarah explained. "Yes, look! Here!" She held up the piece of paper and read out, *"Magyck Crystals for…"* her eyes widened, *"the Protection of the Magyck Curios."* She looked up. "Ava, the curios are *all* magic!"

Ava caught her breath. Right from the start she had sensed there was something strange about the curios but she'd never imagined they might be magical like the crystals. "Oh wow. No wonder Great-Aunt Enid said they were special!"

"I wonder what powers they have?" said Lily, looking at the collection of strange objects on the shelves.

Ava followed her gaze. "Whatever they can do, I'm going to keep their secret and protect them from the world," she said.

"You might also need to protect the world from them," said Sarah. "That crocodile was pretty scary."

"I'll help you," said Lily, linking arms with Ava.

"Me too," said Sarah. "If you want me to, of course," she added uncertainly.

"Definitely," said Ava, linking her other arm through Sarah's. "We'd never have survived today if it wasn't for you." She grinned at Lily. "You were amazing too, Lily. I can't believe you attacked the crocodile with a stick!"

Lily grinned. "It probably wasn't the best idea ever."

"I don't care. It was super brave of you,"

said Ava. She looked happily at them both. "The three of us make an awesome team!"

Pepper stood on her back legs, putting her paws on Ava's thighs, her hazel eyes looking up at her through a fringe.

"OK, the *four* of us," said Ava, grinning. "You were really brave too, Pepper, barking and growling at the crocodile like that – you were grrrrrreat!" The others giggled. Pepper ran to the door and whined hopefully. "I think she wants her tea," said Ava. Her own tummy rumbled loudly. "And she's not the only one. Capturing resurrected mummies is seriously hard work!"

"I could eat a crocodile right now I'm so hungry," agreed Lily.

Ava headed to the door. "Let's go and get some food. I'd like a huge croco-PILE of sandwiches!"

Sarah joined in. "And a hot CROC-olate to drink?"

Chuckling together, they left the room. Pepper was about to follow them when she stopped and looked round, her ears pricking. Clouds had cleared from the full moon outside and now its pale rays were shining through the window, falling on the curios that Ava had just rearranged. A low growl shook the terrier's body as one of the stone objects glowed a faint green. After a few seconds, the glow faded and the stone turned grey again.

Pepper watched for a moment longer and then shook herself and trotted after the girls.

Keep reading for
a sneak peek at the
Magic Keepers' next
adventure...

MAGIC KEEPERS

SPIRIT SURPRISE

CHAPTER ONE

"Magic is real," said Sarah, shaking her head. "Magic is actually real. I still can't believe it."

Ava and Lily grinned at each other. They'd heard Sarah say the same thing at least a hundred times over the last two days – ever since she'd helped them capture an ancient crocodile mummy that had come to life.

Excitement fizzed through Ava. Her life had changed so much since she and her mum had moved into Curio House. The rambling old Victorian villa had once belonged to Enid

Pennington, an archaeologist, but on her death she had left the house and her collection of strange curios to Ava's mum, her great-niece. Ava and her mum had moved in three weeks ago only for Ava to discover something amazing – the curios were magic!

"But how can the rest of the world not know magic exists?" Sarah went on, shifting her school bag on her shoulder as the three of them walked to Ava's house after school on Friday.

Ava shrugged. "I don't know. Maybe because the people who know about it try to keep it secret, like Great-Aunt Enid did."

Lily gave an excited skip, making her dark ponytail bounce. "We're going to keep it secret too, aren't we?"

Ava nodded firmly. The last thing she wanted was for anyone to find out about the magic and take the curios away. There was so much to learn – what magic each curio contained, and what they could do with it…

"Maybe the curios' magic *should* be studied by scientists," said Sarah thoughtfully.

Ava blinked. She knew Sarah loved science but surely she didn't actually want them to tell people?

"Sarah, you're not seriously saying you want us to give up the chance to do magic, are you?" Lily said, looking at her cousin in astonishment.

A grin spread across Sarah's face as she saw Lily and Ava's shocked expressions. "No! But a scientist does need to study them though and that'll be me – starting tonight!"

Ava gave a little skip herself as she thought about the night ahead. Magic and a sleepover with her new friends – what could be better than that?

Curio House was at the top of Fentiman Street, a quiet road lined with houses and cherry trees. The huge, red-brick villa was surrounded by an overgrown walled garden on all sides. Autumn leaves were lying in huge drifts across the lawn and covered the stone steps that led up to the house.

Ava could still hardly believe she and her mum lived there. Their old house had been a cosy, two-bedroom terrace in Nottingham, while Curio House was massive, with nine bedrooms spread over the two top floors. It hadn't been decorated in years and needed a lot of work so Ava's mum Fran was planning on doing it up slowly, starting with the rooms they used most.

When Ava opened the front door, Pepper, her Tibetan terrier, rushed towards them like a hairy black-and-white tornado, her shaggy paws skidding on the wooden floor. Sarah shrank back slightly – she was a bit nervous around dogs.

Ava crouched down. "Have you missed me, Pepper? Yes, I guess you have!" She giggled as Pepper leaped on to her lap and put her front paws on Ava's shoulder. She licked Ava's chin, her dark brown eyes shining through her long fringe. Ava kissed her. Pepper might be very naughty at times but Ava loved her to bits. When she gently pushed her off, Pepper went to say hello to Lily.

"Who's the most beautiful dog in the world? You are, aren't you, Pepper?" Lily cooed. Lily loved all animals, particularly dogs, but she wasn't allowed one because her little brother was allergic to them. After giving Lily several licks, Pepper went over to Sarah.

"Oh, um, hi, Pepper," said Sarah. She looked alarmed as Pepper stood on her back legs and tried to reach Sarah's face with her tongue. "What's she doing?" she said nervously.

"Just saying hello. Come here, Peps," said Ava. "Sarah doesn't want your kisses."

Pepper ignored her.

"Biscuits!" called Ava.

With an excited woof, Pepper gave Sarah's chin a goodbye lick making Sarah giggle, and then she raced to the kitchen doorway and stood there hopefully.

Also by Linda Chapman

Star Friends
NIGHT SHADE

LINDA CHAPMAN
ILLUSTRATED BY LUCY FLEMING

Star Friends
POISON POTION

LINDA CHAPMAN
ILLUSTRATED BY LUCY FLEMING

Star Friends
MOONLIGHT MISCHIEF

LINDA CHAPMAN
ILLUSTRATED BY LUCY FLEMING

Star Friends
HIDDEN CHARM

LINDA CHAPMAN
ILLUSTRATED BY LUCY FLEMING

Dive into all of
the adventures in
Mermaids Rock!

Linda Chapman • Mirelle Ortega

meRMaids ROCK
The Coral Kingdom

Linda Chapman • Mirelle Ortega

meRMaids ROCK
The Floating Forest

Linda Chapman • Mirelle Ortega

meRMaids ROCK
The Ice Giant

Linda Chapman • Mirelle Ortega

meRMaids ROCK
The Midnight Realm

Linda Chapman • Mirelle Ortega

meRMaids ROCK
The Emerald Maze

Linda Chapman • Mirelle Ortega

meRMaids ROCK
The Secret Wreck

ABOUT THE AUTHOR

Linda Chapman is the best-selling author of over 200 books. The biggest compliment Linda can receive is for a child to tell her they became a reader after reading one of her books.

Linda lives in a cottage with a tower in Leicestershire with her husband, three children, three dogs and two ponies. When she's not writing, Linda likes to ride, read and visit schools and libraries to talk to people about writing.

www.lindachapmanauthor.co.uk

ECLIPSE

Alexander Cleave has never been able to rid himself of the feeling that he is being watched —even when alone. So he became an actor, and successfully performed his way through life until suddenly, at the peak of his career, he corpsed in the middle of the last act and staggered off stage, never to return. Self-banished to his childhood home and cut off from his wife, Cleave begins to unravel the past and disinter his own identity. But his attempt to retire, to sift and discard the accumulated clutter of half a century of existence, is undermined by the house itself, brimming with lives, both ghostly and undeniably, robustly human. Memory constantly displaces Cleave's attention to the small, delicate details of the present. So too does his anxiety about the future, and the thought of his beloved but troubled daughter, Cass, tugging away at him like an undertow . . .